RAISING *the* SAIL

RAISING *the*
SAIL

Living in Faith over Fear

Nicole Johnson

W PUBLISHING GROUP

www.wpublishinggroup.com

A Division of Thomas Nelson Inc.
www.ThomasNelson.com

Raising the Sail

Copyright © 2003 Nicole Johnson

Published by W Publishing Group, a Division of Thomas Nelson, Inc., P. O. Box 141000, Nashville, Tennessee 37214.

ISBN 0-8499-1780-8

Printed in the United States of America
03 04 05 06 07 PHX 6 5 4 3 2 1

Contents

For my mother,

with admiration and great joy

The Struggle

I loved her more than words can say.

To give birth to a little girl, to look down at her tiny up-turned nose, to hold her in your arms, is to say a final farewell to your heart. You want to wrap your arms around her small shoulders and squeeze her so tightly that she can't breathe. Your heart simply can't hold all the love you feel—surely it will just burst. There is no way to know at the time how deeply she can break your heart, or how easily you can break hers.

I named her Amy, because it means "beloved."

What is fear before you're a parent? You don't even know how many things there are to be afraid of before you have a child. Ignorance truly is bliss. Yes, love opens you up to joy but simultaneously to fear

that is unending. You lie awake at night surrounded by monsters of possibilities that you've never before considered. Drunk drivers on the street, child molesters in the bathroom, other dysfunctional kids in the neighborhood—the list never ends. What if she misses the bus? Is there a demented man lurking around the school? I hope she doesn't flunk her math test. Not to mention something as horrific as rape—it's bad enough to think about it happening to me, but I only fear landing in the hospital. When I think about it happening to her, I fear landing in prison.

As a mother, are you supposed to just shut all that off? It's impossible. Instead you think on good things and spend your time basking in the joy of watching your little girl discover life. You try to push the fears aside and hope for the best.

So the day I found pills in her backpack, I was at a total loss. The bottom dropped out of my world.

"What are these?" I demanded.

Long pause from my daughter, "Um, I'm not sure."

"You're not sure? They look like pills to me."

"They're not mine." But she wouldn't look at me.

"Whose are they then?"

"Why were you looking in my backpack?"

I wasn't going to let her off. "Whose are they?"

Now she was looking at me. "Why did you go in my backpack?"

"I asked you a question: Who do these belong to?"

"None of your business."

"Then I'm going to assume they're yours. And

you can plan to be home for a while."

"Are you done with my backpack?"

I knew the pills probably belonged to her friend Carlie, but I couldn't be sure. My daughter either had a problem or a loyalty that could become a problem. I had gone into her backpack to get her journal. Okay, I was as embarrassed by that as most mothers are initially, but it didn't stop me. How else was I going to know some things I needed to know? It's justifiable; I'm her mother. And we live in a totally messed-up world. I have to know what's going on in order to protect her. Right?

Fear becomes a cruel master, if you give in to it. In any situation, if you start to obsess over all the things that could go wrong, you go crazy. Like a dog chasing its tail, it is hard to tell who is chasing whom.

You start to see things that aren't really there, your imagination gets the best of you, and you act on those fears. You can drive yourself insane. I should know. I was halfway there.

She never told me the pills were Carlie's, and I was never sure. So I read her emails and listened in on her conversations. The more I tried to get in, the more she shut me out, which made me believe the pills were hers. They were Zoloft and that confused me. I read up on the latest drugs the kids were using and discovered that Zoloft, in combination with another drug, is very popular. Why? What was going on? I was terrified out of my mind.

People liken relationships to being on the water in a sailboat. I've never liked those people. They say things like, "Sailing teaches you to let go and trust."

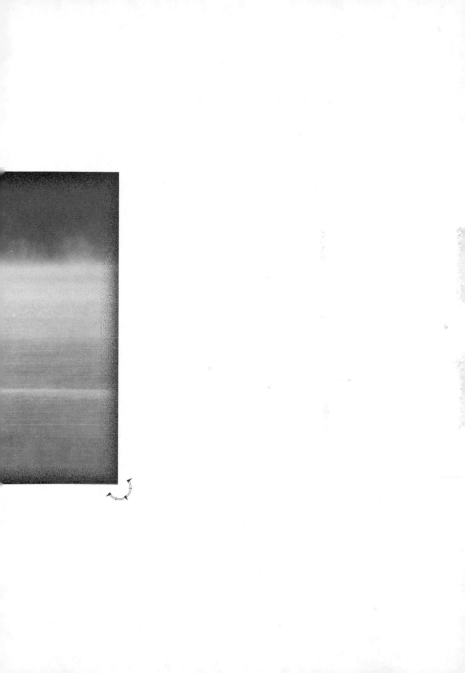

For the record, I've never liked sailing either. I don't want to be out on the water in the middle of nowhere. Besides, you can't always trust. I'm the kind of person that likes to paddle. Or direct things from the dock. Anything but sailing. The wind is maddeningly unpredictable, and you can't control it. I can't think of anything worse than being on the open sea with only a sheet between you and say, Asia.

So there was no sailing, just a lot of spying. Mothers are really good at spying. I can be a regular detective when I need to be—always looking for clues, never settling for what's on the surface, and keeping my eyes and ears open to what's happening around me.

It's fear that leads you to spy rather than ask. Fear prods you to jump to conclusions instead of waiting for clarification. Fear puts a stick in your hand to poke holes in any explanation. Fear whispers that you should mistrust first, and then you can choose to trust later. But by then, all your energy has been spent trying to figure how someone is lying to you. Fear keeps you on the dock.

Amy continued to stay in her own world and made it painfully obvious to me that I wasn't a part of it. Meanwhile, my spying was fruitless. So one afternoon I cut into her world with words sharper than a Ginsu knife. She was on the couch watching TV, silent as usual, and I said, "I washed your clothes, Druggie. Take them to your bedroom."

I saw the cut my words made. She looked me straight in the eye and said, "You are so mean."

I had to look away. "Take your clothes to your bedroom."

My back was to her when she carefully said, "I hate you." It stopped me in my tracks, but I never turned around. "You have to control everything." She was crying now. "You're a control freak, Mother."

I can still hear my laugh. Haughtiness is what fear sounds like when it's laughing. I was at once angry and terrified. *Stand your ground. You're the mother, Maggie. You have the power.* What a joke. The power to do what? To watch my daughter run from me? I was losing her all right, but not for the reasons I thought.

It's not that I believed I was doing everything right, but a control freak? I don't think so. If she was going to label me a control freak because I wanted her to do the right things and grow up into a beautiful young lady, then so be it. As a mother, you can't be out to win a popularity contest. She was the one with the problem. I wasn't the one sneaking around or using drugs. Okay, maybe I was sneaking around, but I had better reasons than she did. And I certainly wasn't using drugs.

And look at what she was doing to my image as a mother. It's not that I thought I would win a perfect mother award, but I had done all the right things in raising her, and now she was singlehandedly taking my name out of the running. If she was doing drugs, what was that saying to all my friends about my parenting skills?

We became like two pieces on a chessboard, moving warily around each other. What she wore, where she went, who her friends were all became bloody battlefields. But we were both losing. I was afraid I couldn't trust her, so I didn't. She certainly didn't trust me, and she avoided me at all costs.

Any faith I'd had that the Lord was working in her life went out the window as fear hijacked my heart. It left me standing on a lonely dock, staring at the cold sea. I was apprehensive about the rising tide, aware of a gathering storm, and sickened by what might lie ahead. I had no idea what to do.

The terrifying thing about being a parent is you can be right and wrong at the very same time. You can do the right things for the wrong reasons or the wrong things for the right reasons. And you can justify anything with, "Because I'm your *mother.*" Looking back, I often punished her because of fear. I was so afraid of what she might be doing. I was afraid of who she might be becoming. But it wasn't until she left home that I became afraid of what I might be doing and who I might be becoming.

"Where are you? Well, put him on the phone... Jim? How did she get there? I want her to come home. I don't care—she belongs here....Well, I'm her mother, and I have full custody...Okay, so drive her back next weekend...Excuse me? Oh, I can? A visit? You have got to be kidding...put her on...She doesn't? That's ridiculous. Jim, I have only been doing what it is my responsibility to do and you know it. She's had issues at school and issues with everything...including me? That was low...No, I don't believe her. I found the pills.... Her grades have dropped. I'm glad you believe her, Jim—you've never had a problem believing anything

people say to you. *Put her on the phone*...I don't care if she's crying. *Put her on the phone*. She said what? Fine. I'll call back tomorrow."

The Storm

You can't exactly choose when you get into the boat. But you know without a doubt when you've tumbled into it. And I was in, like it or not. I had gone from the dock, where I thought I was in control, to being out on the black, choppy water in a vessel I had no idea how to operate. Nothing felt solid, the wind was blowing, and my heart was pounding.

I was angry and fearful and alone. *How dare she?* I sat there, still shaking from the call, thinking, *I'm in the boat now. Are you happy?* talking to no one in particular. I looked around for a paddle. The first clap of an emotional thunderstorm announced its imminent arrival. *So she wants to live with her father. Figures.*

A sure sign that you're a controlling, fearful woman is when the voices in your head are sarcastic. *What kind of stunt is she pulling? Of course she's with her father. The apple never falls far from the tree, does it?* Some people work out with weights, but I get my exercise by jumping to my favorite conclusions. *She loves him and she doesn't love you, Maggie. He's never had to be the bad guy—at least to her.* More thunder overhead and the first few raindrops.

In my mind, I said to her, *It's too bad you can't appreciate everything I've done for you.*

My own voice answered back, *Like the spying and controlling?*

Okay, I was in the boat, like it or not, but I sure as heck didn't have to raise the sail. I glanced at the material tied up in nice little knots on the mast. *Fine, go be with him. You'll probably end up just like him.* Of course she will, she already has, because now she is leaving too. And she would go to Jim. *Why him? Of all the people she could pick, why him?* For ten years, I packed his clothes for trips, I paid the bills while he was gone, I ate dinner every night by myself and washed every pair of his socks fifty-two times. He appreciated it so much he fell in love with someone else and left. *They both had to get away from you, Maggie.*

I stared at the sail all tied up in knots.

The wind was picking up all around me, and the squall was increasing. The drops were coming faster and turning into a torrent. Tears of self-pity began to fall with the water from the sky. *Amy, you won't find*

anybody who loves you more than I do. I could feel the desperation rising like the waves on the water. *Give it a rest, Maggie. You can't call what you've given her love. You never gave it freely and you know it. You drove her away.*

Even if I'd wanted to raise the sail, I couldn't now, because the storm was too intense. *She'll be back,* I thought to myself. But before I finished saying it in my mind, I knew it wasn't true. *Not in a million years. They never come back.* I thought about my own father. *A heart attack at work, he doesn't come home again, and the world is never the same.*

I was raging just like the sea all around me. I screamed into the storm. *No, I don't trust you! Look what it got me in the past. There's too much wind.*

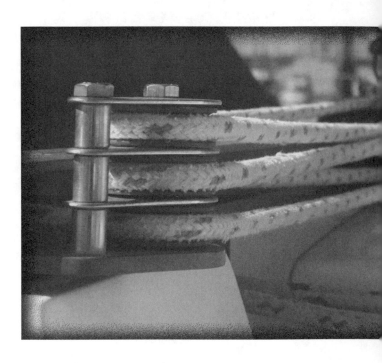

Look at this mess! No father, a husband who runs off, a daughter who hates me, and you want me to let go? Why? So I can drown alone? NO!

It seemed as if the rain was falling sideways in sheets, and the wind was blowing it straight into my face so hard I couldn't see a thing. *What more do you want from me? You've taken everything I had, everything I love.* In my mind's eye, I was a lone figure holding on to the mast and waving my paddle in the face of God. *I can't let go and I can't hold on!*

Just then I heard the voice of God ask gently, "Maggie, what do you want?"

I was sobbing. "I want to yank her out of the street as I did when she was five.

"I want to turn her over my knee.

"I want to hold her in my arms and keep her safe,

but my hands have become claws to her.

"I want to beg her not to leave me.

"I want to say, 'I'm sorry. I'm so sorry. I *am* a control freak.'

"Oh God, help me, I want to change."

The Surrender

I awakened to a glassy sea in the light of the sunrise, full of the pain and peace of surrender. The morning after a storm is infinitely calmer than any ordinary dawn after a quiet night. The contrast must make it so. When daybreak finally appeared after my night on the water, somehow I was different. As they say, what doesn't kill us will make us stronger. My spirit was a white flag blowing in the gentle breeze of the morning. I was tired...weary, but mostly of myself.

The dawn came in more ways than one. I looked at that tied-up sail and knew what I was now free to do. I began to loosen the knots. My deepest struggle was not with my daughter. It was with my own heart. Would I let go and trust God, or would I keep controlling?

At every turn, I wanted to hold on and make her do it my way.

Clearly, this crisis with Amy was just a covering for a deeper question of faith: Did I have any? Would I trust God if He wasn't doing things the way I wanted? Amy had become a pawn in a very holy war. Could I trust God when I couldn't control the outcome? For that matter, could I trust God at all?

The only thing worse than *being* controlling is being *seen* as controlling. No woman wants anyone to think she is a control freak. I'd tried to hide it behind legitimate reasons like love and responsibility. You can hide it until the ones you are "loving" blow the whistle. "Your 'love' is hurting me," they cry. Then they point a finger at the wolf of control dressed in the sheep's

clothing of love. I guess you could say that control is an addiction fed by fear. It's a cheap substitute for real love, like any other drug. I thought I found hers, but actually, she found mine.

How could I have misjudged Amy so harshly? Because I was the one with the problem. I was like the character Lenny in John Steinbeck's novel *Of Mice and Men*. Remember? He was the big simpleton, who just wanted to hold and love the rabbits. And not until they were dead in his hands did he know that he'd held on much too tightly. He just kept holding them and petting them, trying to love them.

God, forgive me.

I took the line holding the main sail and hooked it to the pulley. (I'm sure there are other terms for this, but I'm still learning). Slowly, on deck I was figuring out how to loosen my grip. I'd been holding on too tightly for far too long. And it wasn't just about Amy.

I had always wanted to place all the blame of the failure of our marriage on Jim. I loved to point out all the things I did for him, while remaining silent on the things I didn't do—things like cherish or honor or love. Things that might have been able to save us.

Love comes up from a well in your soul, and for too long my bucket had been hitting bottom and clanging around like a noisy gong. I had nothing to give and I couldn't receive anything from him, either. How long can a man love a woman who refuses to be loved? Break the cycle or it breaks you. It's not that Jim was right, but I will admit it, neither was I.

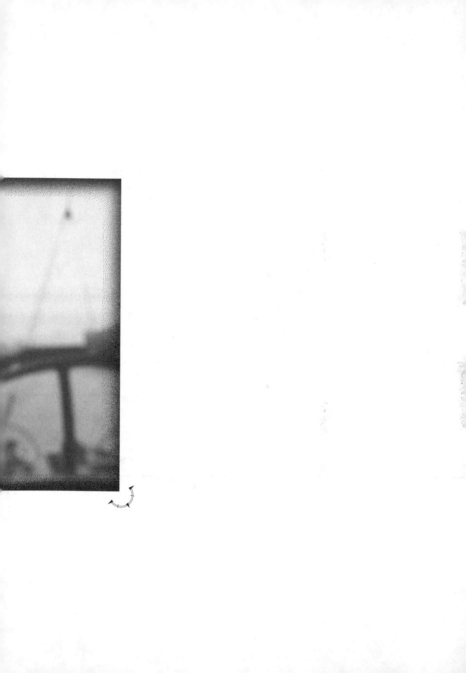

The greatest gift my daughter gave me was to break my heart. My heart had grown too hard and fearful to love. And she split it in two. I became reacquainted with the most incredible six words in human history: "For God so loved the world...." He started it. All of life is a response to His love. We don't have to generate it or think it up or be good enough to get it. We just have to trust it, especially when we can't see it. And that was the problem—I couldn't see it. It didn't appear to me that God had my best interest at heart. I didn't think He was taking care of anything.

I kept thinking, *Amy is going to do the wrong things if I trust her.* In reality, she is going to do the wrong things if I don't trust her. In fact she just might do the wrong things either way—I cannot control that. But—*Lord, have mercy on me a sinner*—I really thought I could. There is such irony in surrender—the thing you fear the most is what you actually should fear the least.

So I got all the knots untied and the sail ready to go. Now I have to keep reminding myself that letting go doesn't tell her I don't care—it shows her that I do. I will let go of her to God. Because He loves her, even more than I do. He wanted to answer Amy's prayers by helping me.

I'm beginning to see my controlling for what it really is. When you are in control of everything, you have to take on the world. From lunch to laundry to love, everything is up to me to fix or finish or follow up. Sure, no one can be responsible for the world, but Maggie the Great was going to die trying. "And in this afternoon's matinee, it's Maggie, in the starring role of God."

God even forgives me for my lousy imperson-ation of Him.

As for Amy, I know I'll have to let her go again and again. *Are you there God?* I'm sure I'll ask when she brings home a new friend who is pierced like a clove-studded ham on Thanksgiving. *God, are You looking after her? Because I'm not above taking this broken paddle and having another go at it.* It will be a daily battle to keep from saying in my heart, *God, You're not doing it right, because she's not following my plan. Oh, God, save me from me.*

It's kind of funny that we can't control our way into being loved more deeply. I'm pretty sure men don't go into a counseling session and say, "I just wish my wife nagged me more." And I know for certain that my daughter will never tell her friends, "My mom doesn't trust me, and I appreciate that." No, in fact, it's just the opposite. The nature of love is trust, even when it is betrayed. Trust is what brings us close. Fear, on the other hand, drives a wedge between us.

Fear is in the very fabric of life, because there is so much that we can't control. Maybe that's why "Do not fear!" is repeated in the Bible over one hundred times. God is constantly telling us not to be afraid, because He knows we almost always are. And for good reasons. But it isn't fear that's the problem; it's what fear makes us do that concerns Him. Somebody said, "Courage is just fear that has said its prayers." I'm saying mine every day.

One thing I've learned is that I'm not the mother I want to be when I sit, trembling, in the dark. Or pace on the dock, waiting for my daughter to come in one minute late so I can demand to smell her breath. I'm not the mother I want to be when I'm swirling out of control in a cyclone of fear. What is going to happen now? *What if…what if…what if…what if…*

I don't want to live that way anymore.

When I kneel by my bed and ask God to look after Amy and trust that He is doing so, I'm choosing faith over fear. But I'm not just trusting her, I'm trusting Him. I am trusting Him with her. At last I'm sailing.

The Sail

*The wind blows wherever it pleases. You hear its sound,
but you cannot tell where it comes from or where it is going.
So it is with everyone born of the Spirit. (John 3:8)*

There is no way to explain how it feels when you finally put up the sail. All of a sudden you realize you are tapping into something that is far bigger than you. Raising the sail sort of feels wrong at first. It's like leaning forward when you're learning to ski. Or being quiet when you want to fill the silence with words. Or calling your daughter to apologize because you've finally seen yourself as you really are. Yielding to the wind runs counter to everything that feels natural.

"I misjudged you horribly, Amy, and I'm sorry. I let fear get the best of me, and it doesn't deserve the best. You do. Will you forgive me?" I thank God every

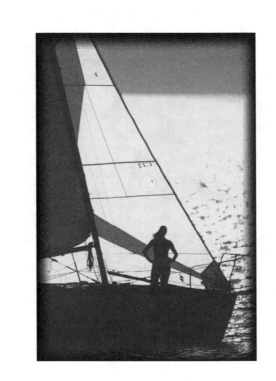

day that Amy wasn't using drugs, but it never really was about that anyway. It was about faith over fear, no matter which way she went.

As soon as the wind takes you, you know it. You can feel it. You are set free and it's exhilarating. I wanted to shout at the top of my lungs, "I'm sailing… I'm sailing!"

You can't clutch, control or seize the wind. You just go where it goes. You turn to and fro, based on whichever way it's moving. So many nights I'd thought I wouldn't survive. But once you've let go, there's peace in the fact that God will be God, with or without you. I could never imagine how freeing that would be. A friend sent me a card that says, "Good morning, I will not be needing your help today. Love, God."

Our ability to control often serves us well—in the ordering of our days, in our multitasking, in our dinner parties. On those occasions, we're not sailing. We just step into a motorboat and get it done. We openly take charge of things and happily run our little worlds. But in the deeper waters of the human heart—when it comes to loving and being loved—only freedom reigns. And there is no beauty like love that is free.

Faith makes us certain of realities that we cannot see. I can't see the sun right now, but I can see the light. I can't see the wind, but I can feel it's there. I take one look up at the sail and there is no doubt. The storms will still come, the fear will still try to overtake me, but faith will sustain me. Faith—at first a gracious gift from God, it then becomes the muscle by which we can keep on trusting. No matter what happens, it is going to be okay. Look at that sail! Asia, here I come!

"Hi, Amy; it's Mom. Of course I'm coming on Saturday...I'll be there around 3:30. Yes...right after my sailing lesson. I know, kinda funny, huh? Because I wanted to. Do you want to go out or stay in for dinner?... It's completely up to you...Of course you know I would prefer to stay—but you know what? I would prefer to do whatever you want to do. Yes, it's me. I'm looking forward to it. I love you too, honey."

More than words can say.

The people who said relationships are like sailing were right. A sailboat is useless when it's fear-bound at the dock. It is made to dip and soar in the breeze, and so is a woman's heart. And when either is running full on, you can't help but notice the power of the wind.

When a woman is trusting God, she is sailing. Her hair is blown about but not her confidence. Her course is set, not by her own agenda, but by the wind of the Spirit. She has thrown the paddle of control overboard, and in faith she raises the sail to let God take her wherever He wants her to go.

She is my Amy, and it means "beloved." Today I'm holding her as I've never held her before. I hold her in my thoughts, and I hold her in my prayers, and I hold her in my heart. And knowing that God is holding me, I have let go. Look at the sail—I'm out of control, and I love it!

About the Author

NICOLE JOHNSON is an actress, writer, and television producer. She is the author of *Fresh Brewed Life* and *Dropping Your Rock*, and is a dramatist with Women of Faith. She makes her home in Santa Monica, California.

The Faith, Hope, and Love Trilogy

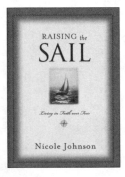

Raising the Sail

Just as sailboats are made for the wind, women are made for relationships, and with both it takes faith to overcome the fear to let go and trust God's direction. Instead of frantically paddling or "motoring" our way through the seas of our emotional connections with each other, she challenges us to freely let go and trust the "Windmaker," God Himself, to help us find our way.

Stepping into the Ring

Where is the woman, old or young, who will not shed a tear but silently scream in her heart as she walks in these pages through the diagnosis of breast cancer and the devastation that ensues? While she focuses on the specific soul-chilling crisis, Nicole offers her readers broader insights for dealing with major losses of all kinds. She extends genuine hope and much-needed rays of light to those who are mired in hopelessness and despair.

Dropping your Rock

You can express your moral outrage by joining the angry mob howling for a sinner to be stoned. But what if that sinner is your friend, and you would rather change her heart than shed her blood? We don't have to hurl the rocks we clutch in our judgmental hands. With tender words and touching photos, Nicole Johnson guides us toward the "flat thud of grace" that can change our lives when we drop our rocks and choose to love instead.

W Publishing Group™
www.wpublishinggroup.com